P9-DHM-573

# RECTANGLE TIME

Words by
**Pamela Paul**

Pictures by
**Becky Cameron**

PHILOMEL

**HA** CASS COUNTY PUBLIC LIBRARY
400 E. MECHANIC
HARRISONVILLE, MO 64701

0 0022 0557422 7

For Zoomer and in memory of Johnny —P. P.

For Rowan and Kiki—my two Rectangle Time accomplices! —B. C.

PHILOMEL BOOKS
An imprint of Penguin Random House LLC, New York

First published in the United States of America by Philomel, an imprint of Penguin Random House LLC, 2021.

Text copyright © 2021 by Pamela Paul.
Illustrations copyright © 2021 by Becky Cameron.

Penguin supports copyright. Copyright fuels creativity, encourages diverse voices, promotes free speech, and creates a vibrant culture. Thank you for buying an authorized edition of this book and for complying with copyright laws by not reproducing, scanning, or distributing any part of it in any form without permission. You are supporting writers and allowing Penguin to continue to publish books for every reader.

Philomel Books is a registered trademark of Penguin Random House LLC.

Visit us online at penguinrandomhouse.com

Library of Congress Cataloging-in-Publication Data is available.

Manufactured in China

ISBN 9780593115114

10 9 8 7 6 5 4 3 2 1

Edited by Liza Kaplan.
Design by Ellice M. Lee.
Text set in Plaintin Std.

Oh, good, it's time! They're bringing out the rectangle.

I know just what they need: a soft, fluffy, non-rectangular shape to offset those sharp corners and round out the company. You can always count on me for Rectangle Time. Be there in a jiff!

Boy, man, rectangle—

and me.

All the necessary pieces are in place.

Here's what I've discovered: Rectangle Time usually takes place at night, though sometimes they break out the rectangle during the day too. The man does a lot of talking, but it's a low-key activity overall. Just the right setting for a furry nuzzle.

Watch carefully: See how the man and the boy
hold the rectangle together? That means they each
have one hand free for me.

You can tell how
much they need me.

Sometimes I scratch an itch on the corner of the rectangle. This is how I help make the rectangle feel useful too.

Other times I rub my signature scent on the rectangle's edges. This is a form of generosity on my part. We all share in our own ways.

Great! It's that time of day again: hello, rectangle!

Wait a second, this is new . . . The boy and the man are
taking turns holding the rectangle now.

That's OK. I'll let whoever's
not holding it stroke my belly.
(Some cats get prickly about the
belly rub. Not me.)

The boy and the man are
taking turns talking too?!
It's nice to have two
voices in the mix.
But three would
be even better.

You know,
background
music.

PURRR
PURRR

Go, Dog.
Go!

Rectangle Time!

Hmmm, something has
seriously shifted. What
happened to the man? Why is
the boy holding the rectangle
all by himself? I better go in.

Look at the poor little guy. He's
just . . . staring at the rectangle.

Alone. Quiet. Too quiet.

Clearly,
he needs me
now more
than ever.

MEOW!

That should break
up the silence. It feels so
good to be helpful.

Phew. He still knows what to do with my chin area. I got worried.

Yes, that's the spot right there; a bit more to the left, please.

To the *left*.

YOW!

Eh, no big deal. It wasn't on purpose. I get it.

Hmm.

That rectangle is awfully small.

No wonder he has to stare at it so hard.

I must be outside his field of vision. I'll just let him know
I'm ready. We all need little reminders sometimes.

Wait, what?

I'm going to
assume that was
an accident.

Ahoy! There's that undersized rectangle again. I'll make things right this time.

Sorry to keep you waiting!
Sweet, fluffy, and very-much-
cuddly object, at your service.

He seems seriously distracted. I'll move a little closer since it's just the two of us these days.

I will . . .

enhance . . .

your rectangle.

Ah, *there* we go.

Now, that was not an accident.

I must be positioning myself wrong.

Maybe softly shaped fluffy objects don't belong on top of rectangles after all. Maybe . . . they belong on top of other irregularly shaped fluffy objects.

There, that's better.

We can still call it Rectangle Time.